RAVEN PENMAN

Moonlit Convergence

First edition

ISBN: 979-8-3304-0927-3

This book was professionally typeset on Reedsy.
Find out more at reedsy.com

Contents

Introduction

As the Harvest Moon cast its silvery glow over Raven Hollow, the town prepared for its most enigmatic festival. The old mansion on the edge of town, long abandoned and whispered about in hushed tones, stood shrouded in mist and mystery. On this Halloween night, three adventurous teenagers—Sarah, Liam, and Emma—dared to explore its darkened halls.

Inside, they discovered an ancient, cryptic book adorned with occult symbols. Unbeknownst to them, their touch triggered an otherworldly signal, opening a rift and drawing alien beings into their midst. As the veil between worlds thinned, the Harvest Moon's light revealed not just shadows, but secrets that would intertwine their fates in ways they could never have anticipated.

Chapter 1: The Mansion

The Harvest Moon loomed large and luminous over Raven Hollow, its pale light casting a spectral sheen across the town's cobblestone streets. The annual Harvest Moon Festival was in full swing, turning the small, fog-covered town into a carnival of ghostly lanterns and ancient traditions. Laughter and music mingled with the crisp autumn air, but a different kind of anticipation thrummed through the town as the moon climbed higher.

At the edge of town, the old mansion stood in stark contrast to the revelry. Its once-grand façade was now cloaked in ivy and shadow, the iron gate sagging on its hinges. The mansion had been abandoned for decades, and local lore painted it as a place of mystery and malevolent spirits. Tonight, it was more than a backdrop for ghost stories; it was a siren call for three daring teenagers.

Sarah, Liam, and Emma approached the mansion with a mix of trepidation and excitement. They were dressed for Halloween— Sarah as a dark enchantress with flowing robes and a hint of arcane mystery, Liam as a swashbuckling rogue with a faux sword at his side, and Emma as a whimsical sprite with shimmering wings. Their costumes were more than mere disguises; they were the masks of their adventurous spirits.

"Are you sure about this?" Liam asked, his voice betraying a nervous edge as he peered through the iron gate. The mansion's silhouette loomed against the moonlit sky like a sleeping giant.

Sarah, holding a flashlight that cut through the fog like a blade, nodded resolutely. "Come on, it's just an old house. What's the worst that could happen?"

Emma, fluttering her wings with a nervous giggle, added, "Besides, it's Halloween. It's supposed to be spooky."

With a shared look of determination, they pushed open the creaking gate and made their way up the overgrown path to the mansion's front door. Each step felt like a step into another world, the sounds of the festival fading into a distant hum.

The front door, adorned with intricate carvings of mythical creatures, was slightly ajar. Sarah pushed it open, and the heavy wood groaned in protest. Inside, the air was thick with dust and the musty scent of neglect. Moonlight filtered through cracked windows, casting ghostly patterns on the faded wallpaper.

"Wow," Liam said, his voice echoing in the empty hall. "This place is straight out of a horror movie."

Sarah led the way, her flashlight sweeping over the dilapidated grandeur of the mansion. The grand staircase, though crumbling, still hinted at its former elegance. Ancient portraits with eyes that seemed to follow their every move lined the walls, and chandeliers, long bereft of their crystals, hung like skeletal remains from the ceiling.

In the dim light, Emma's attention was drawn to a door slightly ajar, leading to a large parlor. "Look over there," she whispered, her curiosity piqued.

Inside the parlor, amidst broken furniture and scattered debris, stood an ornate pedestal with a large, dusty book resting on it. The book's cover was adorned with strange, intricate symbols that seemed to pulse faintly under the beam of Sarah's flashlight.

"This looks old," Sarah said, her eyes widening with intrigue. "Let's see what it is."

Liam and Emma crowded around as Sarah carefully lifted the book. Its weight was surprising, and the pages felt brittle under her touch. The symbols on the cover seemed to shimmer in the light, almost as if they were alive.

"What do you think it's about?" Liam asked, peering over Sarah's shoulder.

"I'm not sure," Sarah replied, her fingers brushing over the symbols. "But it looks like it could be some kind of occult text."

Without warning, the room was filled with a low, humming vibration that seemed to resonate with the symbols on the book. The air grew heavy, and a strange, pulsating light began to seep through the cracks in the walls.

"What's happening?" Emma exclaimed, her wings fluttering anxiously.

Before anyone could respond, the ground trembled, and the book opened on its own, the pages flipping rapidly as if caught in a storm. The symbols began to glow with an eerie, greenish light, and the room filled with an otherworldly energy.

A rift appeared in the air, its edges shimmering like liquid light. From within the rift, shadowy forms began to emerge, their shapes both alien and unsettling.

Sarah, Liam, and Emma stared in stunned silence as the first of the alien beings stepped through, their forms cloaked in an ethereal, greenish hue. The rift began to close behind them, and the room's atmosphere crackled with an unknown force.

The teenagers were frozen, caught between the familiar comfort of their Halloween night and the surreal reality of what they had just unleashed. The mansion's curse had been stirred, and the Harvest Moon's light had revealed more than just shadows.

As the aliens took shape and the light of the rift faded, Sarah's heart raced. Tonight was no longer about a thrill-seeking adventure; it was about surviving the consequences of awakening an ancient power.

Chapter 2: The Rift

The room fell into a tense silence, broken only by the soft, disorienting hum that filled the air. Sarah, Liam, and Emma stood rooted to the spot, their eyes wide with disbelief as the alien beings materialized from the rift. The once-grand parlor, now a stage for otherworldly events, seemed to shrink under the weight of the incomprehensible scene before them.

The aliens, their forms shadowy and indistinct, moved with an eerie grace. They were tall and slender, their skin a shifting, translucent green that pulsed with an internal light. Their eyes, though largely concealed by the shadows of their hoods, glowed with an unsettling, intelligence. The air grew colder, the temperature dropping with every step they took.

"Are those… aliens?" Liam's voice trembled, his hand gripping Emma's shoulder for support. His usual bravado was nowhere to be found in the face of this cosmic horror.

Emma's eyes were wide, her earlier excitement replaced by genuine fear. "I don't know what they are, but they're definitely not from around here."

Sarah, the most composed of the trio despite her racing heart, took a cautious step forward. Her fingers hovered over the symbols in the book, which had now settled into a soft, pulsing glow. "We need to figure out what this means. There has to be something in the book that explains what's happening."

Before she could open the book, one of the aliens, seemingly the leader, stepped forward. Its presence was commanding, its eyes fixated on the book. The alien's voice, though incomprehensible at first, soon resonated with an eerie clarity, as though spoken directly into their minds.

"Beware," it intoned, the sound both haunting and oddly melodious. "The ritual has begun."

The words echoed in their minds, sending a shiver down Sarah's spine. She glanced at Liam and Emma, their faces reflecting a shared anxiety. They needed to act quickly.

The alien continued, its voice a blend of authority and sorrow. "We are bound by a curse that ties us to this realm until the ritual is completed. The book is a key, and you have awakened it."

Sarah's mind raced. She had read about rituals and curses in her occult studies, but this was beyond anything she had encountered. "What kind of ritual? What do you want from us?"

The alien's gaze softened, revealing a flicker of empathy. "We seek an artifact that holds the power to break our curse. It lies hidden within this mansion, and it must be retrieved before the alignment of the Harvest Moon is complete."

Liam's eyes darted around the room, searching for any clues. "So, we have to help you find this artifact?"

The alien's eyes flashed with a strange, hopeful light. "You must assist us, or the curse will bind us—and your world—to a fate worse than death."

Sarah took a deep breath, her mind already working through the implications. If they didn't help, there was no telling what could happen. "Alright. We'll help you find this artifact. But if we're going to do this, we need to know more. Where should we start looking?"

The alien leader extended a slender hand towards the book. "The book holds the map to the artifact's location. But be warned, the mansion is filled with traps and illusions meant to protect the artifact."

Emma's gaze was fixed on the book, her anxiety momentarily replaced by determination. "We need to be careful. If the mansion is as dangerous as they say, we could be walking into a trap ourselves."

With a nod of agreement, Sarah opened the book again. The pages, though worn and fragile, revealed a series of maps and symbols. The symbols matched those on the walls of the mansion, indicating that the mansion itself was a labyrinth designed to protect the artifact. Sarah's heart raced as she deciphered the text. The artifact was hidden in a chamber deep within the mansion, accessible only through a series of intricate puzzles and hidden passages.

The alien leader's form shimmered slightly as it extended a hand towards the book. "Follow the path outlined within. The mansion's defenses are formidable, but you are not alone. We will guide you."

As Sarah, Liam, and Emma began their search, they felt a sudden rush of cold air. The mansion seemed to come alive around them, its walls shifting and changing. The lights flickered, casting long, menacing shadows that seemed to whisper threats. The familiar, comforting aura of Halloween was replaced by an overwhelming sense of dread.

The trio moved cautiously through the mansion, their footsteps echoing in the empty halls. The book's instructions led them to a series of hidden doors and passages, each more perplexing than the last. They encountered traps—pressure plates that triggered hidden darts, walls that closed in with grinding sounds, and illusions that distorted their perception of reality.

Despite the danger, they pressed on, their determination fueled by the urgency of their task. The mansion seemed to test their resolve at every turn, challenging their courage and wits. Sarah's knowledge of occult magic and Liam's quick thinking proved invaluable as they navigated the mansion's treacherous maze.

As they reached what appeared to be the final chamber, the

air grew heavy with anticipation. The chamber was vast and adorned with intricate carvings that glowed faintly in the moonlight. In the center of the chamber stood a pedestal, upon which rested a small, ornate box. The artifact was within reach, but the chamber was guarded by a final puzzle—one that required both their knowledge and their unity.

Sarah, Liam, and Emma worked together, deciphering the symbols and solving the riddles that guarded the box. Their combined efforts finally led them to the solution, and the box opened with a soft, resonant chime.

Inside was a crystal orb, its surface shimmering with an inner light. The artifact they had sought, and the key to breaking the curse, was finally in their hands.

As they prepared to return to the parlor, where the aliens awaited, they couldn't shake the feeling that their journey was far from over. The mansion had tested them, but the true challenge lay ahead. They were not just aiding the aliens; they were also facing a destiny that would intertwine their fates with forces beyond their understanding.

The Harvest Moon shone brightly outside, its light casting a hopeful glow on their path. But the night was still young, and the final outcome remained uncertain. With the artifact in hand, they faced the next chapter of their adventure, knowing that the balance between their world and the alien realm was about to shift in ways they could scarcely imagine.

Chapter 3: The Cursed Convergence

With the artifact—a crystal orb glowing with an inner light—clutched tightly in Sarah's hands, the trio retraced their steps through the labyrinthine mansion. Each creak of the floorboards and distant echo seemed to amplify their growing anxiety. The mansion's oppressive atmosphere, combined with the weight of their task, made every shadow seem more menacing.

As they navigated their way back, the mansion itself seemed to resist their progress. Walls shifted subtly, passages twisted, and an unnerving silence blanketed the once bustling corridors. The trio could feel the mansion's ancient magic at work, testing their resolve and threatening to lead them astray.

"Do you think we're being watched?" Emma's voice was barely a whisper, her eyes darting around nervously.

"Definitely," Liam replied, his hand resting on the hilt of his prop sword, which offered little actual protection. "This place is trying to mess with us."

Sarah, focusing on the book's cryptic instructions, guided them through the maze. Her heart pounded with a mixture of fear and determination. The symbols on the book had grown more complex as they neared their destination, their meanings intertwined with the mansion's dark magic.

"Keep your eyes open," Sarah said. "We're close to the parlor. Once we get there, we need to act quickly."

The parlor was no longer the dusty, forgotten room they had first encountered. The air was charged with an ominous energy, and the ambient light seemed to pulse in rhythm with the orb's glow. The alien beings awaited them, their forms casting long shadows that danced eerily along the walls.

The leader alien, its presence as commanding as ever, stepped forward as they entered. Its eyes, though still partially obscured by shadow, locked onto the crystal orb with a mix of relief and urgency. "You have retrieved the artifact. The ritual can now proceed."

Sarah took a deep breath, feeling a wave of fatigue and apprehension. "How do we use it to break the curse?"

The alien leader extended a slender hand toward the pedestal where the book had previously rested. "Place the orb on the pedestal. It will activate the ritual, but be warned: the ritual's energy will resonate with the mansion's magic. It will test your willpower and your unity."

Liam glanced at Sarah and Emma, their faces illuminated by the orb's soft light. "Let's get this done."

Sarah carefully placed the orb on the pedestal. As it made contact, the room filled with a brilliant, pulsating light. The carvings on the walls began to glow, and the mansion itself seemed to tremble in response. The very air crackled with a blend of anticipation and dread.

A series of symbols and sigils emerged from the walls, swirling around the orb in an intricate dance of light and shadow. The alien leader began to chant in a language that was both haunting and rhythmic. The chant resonated through the chamber, its vibrations harmonizing with the orb's pulsating light.

The energy from the ritual began to interact with the mansion's magic. The walls shifted, revealing hidden passages and traps that had lain dormant. The mansion seemed to come alive, its ancient defenses awakening in an attempt to thwart the ritual.

Sarah, Liam, and Emma fought to stay focused. The mansion's enchantments were powerful, manifesting as illusions and physical barriers designed to disorient and separate them. Shadows twisted into threatening shapes, and the temperature fluctuated wildly, creating an environment that was both physically and mentally taxing.

Emma stumbled as the ground beneath her seemed to buckle, but Liam caught her just in time. "Stay close," he urged. "We need to stick together."

As the ritual progressed, the energy from the orb began to interact with the curse that had bound the aliens. The air grew heavier with each passing moment, and the mansion's defenses grew more intense. The symbols on the walls shifted, forming complex patterns that seemed to pulse with a malevolent intelligence.

Sarah, with her knowledge of occult magic, worked alongside the alien leader to decipher the shifting symbols. They needed to align the energies of the orb with the mansion's magic precisely to break the curse. The process was exhausting, requiring not only mental acuity but also a deep emotional connection between the participants.

The trio's unity was tested as never before. The mansion's magic played on their fears and insecurities, manifesting their deepest anxieties. Sarah saw visions of failure and loss, while Liam was plagued by doubts about his courage. Emma experienced overwhelming feelings of inadequacy, amplified by the mansion's dark magic.

Despite the overwhelming odds, they pressed on. Their shared determination and their commitment to helping the aliens pushed them through the darkest moments. The orb's light grew brighter, pushing back the shadows and dispelling the illusions that sought to break their spirit.

The chant of the alien leader reached a crescendo, and the symbols on the walls converged into a single, blinding sigil. The chamber was bathed in an intense, purifying light that pushed back the mansion's malevolent forces. The curse's grip on the aliens began to wane, its influence weakening as the ritual reached its climax.

With one final, resonant chant, the ritual was complete. The orb's light subsided, and the mansion's defenses began to retract. The oppressive atmosphere lifted, replaced by a profound sense of relief and calm.

The alien leader, its form shimmering with a newfound clarity, approached Sarah, Liam, and Emma. "The curse has been broken. We are free to return to our realm."

Sarah felt a wave of exhaustion and triumph wash over her. "We did it. But what now?"

The alien leader's eyes, filled with gratitude, conveyed a silent message of farewell. "Your world is safe for now. The bond between our realms has been temporarily restored. Should we meet again, it will be under different circumstances."

With that, the aliens began to shimmer and fade, their forms dissolving into the ambient light of the Harvest Moon. The rift closed, and the mansion's oppressive energy dissipated.

Sarah, Liam, and Emma stood together in the now-quiet parlor, the weight of their experience settling over them. The mansion, once a place of fear and mystery, was now just a relic of an extraordinary night.

As they made their way outside, the first light of dawn began to break over the horizon. The town of Raven Hollow was beginning to stir, its Halloween festivities winding down. The trio looked back at the mansion, its dark silhouette now a mere shadow against the morning sky.

They had faced an unimaginable challenge and emerged victorious. The bond forged between them during the night's trials had strengthened their friendship and revealed their inner strength. The Harvest Moon had witnessed a convergence of worlds and a story that would remain etched in their memories forever.

Chapter 4: The Aftermath

The first light of dawn crept over Raven Hollow, its golden rays slowly dispelling the lingering shadows of the night. The Harvest Moon had faded into a memory, leaving behind a sense of quiet and calm. The once-ominous mansion stood silent at the edge of town, its dark allure now subdued by the morning sun.

Sarah, Liam, and Emma emerged from the mansion, their costumes disheveled and their faces etched with exhaustion. They were greeted by the sight of the town's awakening—children running through the streets with candy bags, parents chatting and cleaning up from the festivities. The contrast between the mundane cheeriness of the town and the extraordinary events they had just experienced felt almost surreal.

"I can't believe it's over," Emma said, her voice tinged with both relief and disbelief. "It feels like a dream."

Liam nodded, his expression a mix of awe and fatigue. "Yeah, one hell of a Halloween night. I never thought we'd actually come face-to-face with aliens."

Sarah glanced back at the mansion, its once-menacing silhouette now softened by the morning light. "It's strange. The mansion doesn't feel the same. It's like the magic that was holding it together has dissipated."

The trio walked back toward the center of town, their footsteps echoing in the quiet streets. The events of the previous night had forged a bond between them—one that was both deep and transformative. They had faced fear and uncertainty together, and their shared experience had brought them closer.

As they reached the town square, they noticed a group of familiar faces approaching them. It was their friends and fellow festival-goers, who had been curious about their absence.

"There you guys are!" called out Ben, a friend from school. "We were worried. Where have you been?"

Sarah hesitated, her mind racing for a plausible explanation. "We… got caught up exploring the old mansion. It turned out to be more than we bargained for."

Ben's eyes widened, but before he could ask more, Emma interjected with a quick smile. "We had a bit of an adventure, but we're fine now. Just needed some time to get back."

Their friends seemed to accept the vague explanation, and the conversation soon shifted to the aftermath of the festival. Sarah, Liam, and Emma were relieved to divert attention from the strange and otherworldly events of the night.

As the day wore on, the trio found themselves gathered at a small café, seeking solace in warm drinks and comfort food. The atmosphere was cozy, a stark contrast to the eerie ambiance of the mansion.

"Do you think the town will ever find out what really happened?" Liam asked, stirring his coffee absentmindedly.

Sarah shook her head. "I don't think so. The mansion's magic was too ancient and hidden. The ritual might have created a temporary rift, but it's closed now. The town will probably just chalk it up to Halloween excitement."

Emma sipped her hot chocolate thoughtfully. "I hope so. I don't think anyone would believe the truth. Besides, we did what we needed to do."

As they spoke, Sarah's thoughts turned to the alien leader and the otherworldly encounter. The brief connection they had shared had been profound, but the reality of their departure left her with a lingering sense of wonder and melancholy.

"I keep thinking about the aliens," Sarah said. "Their gratitude and the way they spoke about the curse… it was like they were genuinely relieved to be free."

Liam nodded. "Yeah, it was like they were stuck between worlds, and we helped them find their way back."

Emma looked out the window, her gaze thoughtful. "Maybe it was more than just a Halloween adventure. Maybe it was a reminder that there's more to the universe than we can see."

As the sun climbed higher in the sky, the trio continued to reflect on their experiences. The mansion was now a silent, enigmatic relic of their extraordinary night, and the Harvest Moon had set behind them, its light replaced by the clarity of day.

Their friendship had been tested and strengthened, and they knew that the events of the night would always be a part of them. They had faced an ancient curse and witnessed a convergence of worlds, and their lives had been forever altered.

The day passed with a sense of quiet resolution. The town of Raven Hollow returned to its ordinary rhythm, the Halloween festivities fading into the background of everyday life. Yet, for Sarah, Liam, and Emma, the night's events remained vivid—a testament to their bravery and the mysteries that lay beyond the veil of the known.

As twilight approached and the day drew to a close, the trio parted ways, each carrying with them the weight and wonder of their shared adventure. They knew that their lives had been touched by something extraordinary, and they looked forward to the future with a newfound sense of wonder and possibility.

The mansion, now a mere silhouette against the evening sky, stood as a silent witness to the night's events. The curses had been broken, the ritual completed, and the balance between worlds restored. Yet, in the quiet aftermath, the mansion's secrets remained, waiting for the next chapter in its enigmatic history.

Sarah, Liam, and Emma walked away from the café, their paths diverging as they ventured into their separate lives. But the bond they had formed and the lessons they had learned would remain with them, a reminder of the extraordinary adventure that had unfolded beneath the light of the Harvest Moon.

Chapter 5: Echoes of the Past

Weeks had passed since the Halloween night that had forever altered the lives of Sarah, Liam, and Emma. Raven Hollow had returned to its usual pace, the excitement of the Harvest Moon fading into the routine of daily life. The trio had resumed their regular activities, but the shadows of their adventure still lingered in their minds.

Sarah was in the local library, her refuge for contemplation and research. The experience at the mansion had left her with an insatiable curiosity about the occult and the cosmic forces she had encountered. She had spent countless hours researching ancient texts, hoping to understand more about the magic she had briefly wielded.

She was flipping through a tome on ancient curses when she felt a presence behind her. Turning, she saw Liam and Emma approaching, their faces reflecting a mix of concern and curiosity.

"Hey, Sarah," Liam greeted, taking a seat beside her. "We were wondering if you've found anything new about what happened."

Sarah looked up, her expression thoughtful. "Actually, yes. I've been digging into the history of the mansion and the symbols we saw. It turns out the mansion was built on ley lines—powerful energy lines that intersect across the world. That might explain why it was a focal point for such intense magical activity."

Emma, who had joined them at the table, looked intrigued. "Ley lines? That sounds like something out of a fantasy novel."

"It's more real than you might think," Sarah said, nodding. "Many ancient cultures believed that these energy lines had significant power. The mansion's location on these lines might have made it a magnet for mystical forces."

As they spoke, Sarah's mind kept drifting back to the aliens and the artifact. The sense of unfinished business was strong. Despite their victory over the curse, the experience had left her with lingering questions about the nature of the artifact and the alien realm.

"I've been thinking about the crystal orb," Sarah continued. "We never learned what happened to it after the ritual. The aliens took it with them when they left."

Liam leaned in, his curiosity piqued. "You don't think there's a chance they might come back, do you?"

Sarah shrugged, her brow furrowed. "I don't know. The alien leader seemed certain that their curse was broken, but there's always a chance they could return, especially if there's more at stake than we realized."

Emma looked contemplative. "Maybe the mansion isn't completely done with us yet. There might be more to discover, or more consequences from what we did."

As the trio discussed their thoughts, a sudden gust of wind blew through the library, causing the pages of Sarah's book to flutter. The air seemed to shimmer momentarily, and a strange, almost imperceptible hum filled the room.

Sarah looked up, her eyes scanning the library. "Did anyone else feel that?"

Liam and Emma exchanged puzzled glances. "Felt like a breeze," Liam said.

Sarah's sense of unease grew. She had learned to be attuned to magical disturbances, and this felt distinctly unusual. "I think we should check out the mansion again."

The suggestion was met with a mixture of apprehension and agreement. They hadn't returned to the mansion since the ritual, and the idea of revisiting it stirred both curiosity and unease.

That afternoon, the trio made their way back to the mansion, their footsteps echoing on the gravel path. The mansion loomed before them, its exterior appearing less menacing in the daylight but still shrouded in an aura of ancient mystery.

The front door, now slightly ajar, seemed to beckon them inside. Sarah led the way, her flashlight cutting through the dimness of the entrance hall. The mansion felt different, quieter, as if holding its breath.

As they moved through the familiar corridors, they noticed subtle changes. The oppressive atmosphere of the previous visit had lifted, replaced by an eerie calm. The once-vibrant symbols on the walls were now faded and almost imperceptible.

They made their way back to the parlor where they had performed the ritual. The pedestal where the crystal orb had rested was now empty. The air was still, and the chamber felt strangely devoid of the intense magical energy they had experienced before.

Emma's gaze wandered around the room. "Everything seems… different. Like the magic has settled down."

Sarah approached the pedestal, examining the area closely. "The orb might have been more significant than we thought. There could be residual effects from its presence."

Just as she was about to turn away, Liam's eyes caught sight of something unusual. "Hey, look at this."

He pointed to a small, hidden compartment in the wall, barely noticeable unless you knew where to look. It had been concealed by a panel that seemed to blend seamlessly with the surrounding wall.

Sarah's heart raced as she approached the compartment. With a careful touch, she opened it, revealing a small, intricately carved box. It was covered in the same symbols they had seen in the mansion's magical defenses.

"This looks important," Sarah said, her voice tinged with excitement. "Let's see what's inside."

She opened the box, revealing a collection of old scrolls and a single, dusty tome. The tome's cover was adorned with the same alien symbols they had encountered during the ritual.

Liam and Emma leaned in, their curiosity piqued. "What do you think it is?" Emma asked.

Sarah gently opened the tome, her eyes scanning the ancient text. "It looks like a journal of some sort. It might contain information about the mansion, the ritual, and the artifact."

As she read through the journal, Sarah's eyes widened. The journal detailed the history of the mansion, its construction, and the powerful magic it had once held. It also included entries about the curse placed on the aliens and their role in guarding the artifact.

"This journal explains a lot," Sarah said, her voice filled with awe. "It seems the mansion was a crucial point of intersection for various mystical forces. The alien curse was just one part of a larger cosmic balance."

Liam and Emma listened intently as Sarah read excerpts from the journal. It spoke of ancient beings, powerful artifacts, and the delicate balance between worlds. The information painted a picture of a universe far more complex and interconnected than they had ever imagined.

As they delved deeper into the journal, they found a final entry that stood out. It mentioned the possibility of a new alignment, a shift that could bring further changes to the mansion and its magical properties.

Sarah's mind raced with possibilities. "If this alignment is approaching, it could mean more disturbances or even new visitors from other realms. We need to be prepared."

The trio left the mansion with a renewed sense of purpose. The discoveries they had made were both fascinating and daunting, hinting at further adventures and challenges. They knew that the mansion's secrets were far from fully uncovered and that their journey was far from over.

As they walked back to town, the setting sun cast long shadows, and the air was filled with a sense of quiet anticipation. The echoes of the past were still resonating, and the future held unknown possibilities. For Sarah, Liam, and Emma, the mansion had become more than just a place of haunting memories—it was a gateway to a broader, more enigmatic universe.

They parted ways that evening, each contemplating the implications of their newfound knowledge. The mansion's mysteries had only just begun to unfold, and the echoes of the past promised to guide them on their continuing journey through the unknown.

Chapter 6: Unseen Forces

The weeks that followed were a blur of research and preparation for Sarah, Liam, and Emma. The journal they had discovered revealed tantalizing clues about the mansion's ancient role as a nexus of mystical energy. Each entry deepened their understanding of the complex web of magic that intertwined their world with realms beyond their comprehension.

Sarah spent hours poring over the journal, cross-referencing its entries with historical records and other occult texts. She meticulously documented every symbol, every spell, and every reference to the ley lines that intersected at the mansion. Her once peaceful library now looked like an epicenter of mystical investigation, with papers strewn across tables and arcane symbols sketched on every available surface.

Emma, ever the practical one, took on the task of ensuring they were prepared for any new developments. She researched protective charms and wards, seeking ways to shield themselves from potential magical disturbances. Her apartment was cluttered with herbs, crystals, and various magical artifacts she'd acquired.

Liam, meanwhile, focused on physical readiness. He practiced with his prop sword and trained in basic self-defense, determined to be prepared for any physical threats they might encounter. He also took on the role of coordinating their efforts, keeping track of their progress and ensuring that their research didn't become overwhelming.

Despite their individual efforts, they remained united in their goal. Their bond, forged through the trials of the mansion, was stronger than ever. They knew that whatever challenges lay ahead, they would face them together.

One crisp autumn evening, the trio gathered at Sarah's house to review their findings. The air was cool, and the leaves outside rustled softly in the breeze. Inside, the atmosphere was charged with a sense of anticipation.

Sarah spread out the journal's pages and her research notes on the table. "I think we've uncovered something significant. According to the journal, the mansion's alignment with the ley lines has been stable for centuries, but it's due for a new cosmic alignment soon. This could trigger additional disturbances or even attract new entities."

Emma looked up from her notes, her expression serious. "We need to be prepared for anything. The journal mentioned a ritual that could either stabilize the mansion's magic or further destabilize it. We should consider performing the ritual ourselves, just to be safe."

Liam nodded in agreement. "If the ritual could help us manage the magical energy, it might prevent any more surprises."

Sarah glanced at the journal, her fingers tracing a particularly intricate symbol. "The ritual involves creating a protective barrier around the mansion using a combination of ancient symbols and natural elements. It's complex, but I think we can manage it with the right preparations."

The trio spent the next few days gathering the necessary components for the ritual. They collected rare herbs, crafted protective charms, and carefully prepared the symbols that would form the barrier. The process was arduous but necessary, and their efforts were marked by a sense of urgency and purpose.

As the night of the ritual approached, the mansion stood as a silent sentinel against the backdrop of the Harvest Moon. The town of Raven Hollow was oblivious to the preparations unfolding behind its walls, the eerie calm of the mansion belying the energy it contained.

On the night of the ritual, Sarah, Liam, and Emma arrived at the mansion under the cover of darkness. The moonlight illuminated their path as they carried their supplies and prepared for the task ahead. The mansion seemed to hold its breath, as if aware of the significance of their visit.

They entered the mansion and made their way to the parlor, where they had performed the previous ritual. The room was prepared with the symbols and artifacts they had collected. Sarah took the lead, carefully arranging the symbols on the floor according to the instructions in the journal.

Liam and Emma set up protective wards around the room, their movements precise and methodical. The atmosphere was tense, and the air seemed charged with an electric anticipation.

As they completed their preparations, Sarah took a deep breath and began the ritual. She chanted the incantations from the journal, her voice steady despite the eerie silence that enveloped them. The symbols on the floor began to glow, and a soft, resonant hum filled the room.

The ritual's energy interacted with the mansion's magic, creating a protective barrier that shimmered with a faint, ethereal light. The room seemed to vibrate with a new sense of stability, and the oppressive atmosphere that had once pervaded the mansion began to lift.

Suddenly, a gust of wind rushed through the room, and the air was filled with a low, resonant sound. The light of the barrier intensified, casting strange, shifting shadows on the walls. The mansion seemed to respond to the ritual, its ancient magic aligning with the new protective energies.

Sarah, Liam, and Emma stood together, their eyes fixed on the glowing barrier. They felt a profound sense of accomplishment and relief. The ritual appeared to be working, and the mansion's magic was being stabilized.

As the ritual neared its completion, a figure appeared in the doorway. It was an old man, his face lined with age and wisdom.

He wore a long, flowing robe adorned with intricate symbols, and his presence exuded an aura of authority and knowledge.

The trio turned, their eyes widening in surprise. "Who are you?" Sarah asked, her voice steady despite her shock.

The old man smiled, his eyes twinkling with a knowing light. "I am the keeper of the mansion's secrets," he said. "You have done well to perform the ritual and restore balance. The mansion's magic is now stabilized, and the cosmic alignment will proceed without further disturbances."

Sarah, Liam, and Emma exchanged relieved glances. "We were just trying to ensure that the magic remained under control," Liam said.

The old man nodded. "You have succeeded. The mansion's role as a nexus of magical energy has been preserved, and its secrets will remain safe for now. But remember, the universe is vast and full of mysteries. Your journey may have just begun."

With that, the old man turned and vanished into the shadows, leaving the trio alone in the parlor. The barrier's light dimmed, and the room returned to its former state of quiet calm.

The three friends left the mansion with a renewed sense of purpose. Their actions had preserved the balance of the mansion's magic, but the old man's words lingered in their minds. The universe held countless secrets, and their adventure had only scratched the surface.

As they walked away from the mansion, the dawn began to break over Raven Hollow. The town stirred with the promise of a new day, and the trio looked forward to the future with a sense of excitement and wonder.

Their bond had been tested and strengthened, and they knew that their journey was far from over. The mansion had revealed its secrets, but the mysteries of the universe awaited them.

They parted ways, each contemplating the possibilities that lay ahead. The echoes of their adventure would guide them, and the future held endless potential. The Harvest Moon had marked the beginning of a new chapter, and their story was just beginning.

Chapter 7: The Cosmic Convergence

Months had passed since the ritual at the mansion, and life in Raven Hollow had returned to a semblance of normalcy. Sarah, Liam, and Emma had resumed their routines, but the impact of their extraordinary experience lingered in their thoughts and actions. They had resumed their studies and hobbies, yet the universe seemed to keep its mysterious allure just out of reach.

One crisp, clear night, Sarah found herself lying awake in bed, staring at the star-studded sky through her window. The Harvest Moon had long set, but the cosmos seemed to whisper secrets that beckoned her. Her mind buzzed with fragments of the old man's final words: "The universe is vast and full of mysteries."

Driven by an insatiable curiosity, Sarah had continued her research into cosmic alignments and ley lines. She had discovered that an extraordinary celestial event was approaching—a rare alignment of planets that would open a temporary rift between worlds. The event was set to occur in just a few days, and she couldn't shake the feeling that it might be connected to their previous encounter.

Unable to ignore the pull of her intuition, Sarah decided to consult Liam and Emma. She knew they had shared the same sense of wonder and responsibility, and she needed their support for what might lie ahead.

The trio gathered at Sarah's house late one evening, their faces illuminated by the soft glow of lamps and the shimmering light of the stars visible through the windows.

"I've been researching the upcoming planetary alignment," Sarah began, her voice tinged with excitement. "It's a rare event that happens once in several centuries. According to my sources, it could open a rift between our world and others. I think it might be related to the mansion and the cosmic balance we worked to restore."

Liam looked intrigued, leaning forward in his chair. "So, what does this mean for us? Are we expecting more disturbances?"

"It's hard to say," Sarah admitted. "But given the mansion's role as a nexus of magical energy, it might be crucial to understand and manage any potential rifts that form. We need to be prepared for whatever might come through."

Emma nodded thoughtfully. "If the alignment could create a rift, we should consider how to protect ourselves and the town. Do you have any ideas on how we might handle it?"

Sarah pulled out a map she had been working on, marking the locations of ley lines and significant points of magical interest. "We need to observe the alignment closely and see if any anomalies occur. If a rift opens, we may have to perform a containment ritual similar to what we did before, but it will likely need to be adapted for this new situation."

The trio spent the following days preparing for the celestial event. They gathered additional magical supplies, reinforced their protective charms, and studied the ancient texts related to cosmic alignments. The anticipation of the alignment added a sense of urgency to their preparations.

On the night of the planetary alignment, the sky was a breathtaking spectacle of celestial bodies. The planets aligned in a rare formation, casting a unique, ethereal glow across the night sky. Sarah, Liam, and Emma stood on a hill overlooking the town, their eyes fixed on the heavens.

The atmosphere was charged with a palpable sense of energy, and the air felt electric with possibility. As the planets reached their peak alignment, the first signs of a rift began to manifest. A faint, shimmering distortion appeared in the air, stretching and pulsing with the rhythm of the celestial bodies.

"We need to act quickly," Sarah said, her voice steady despite the awe and tension in the air. "The rift is forming. Let's prepare the containment ritual."

They hurried to set up their ritual space, carefully arranging symbols and artifacts to create a protective barrier. The ritual was complex, requiring precise timing and coordination. Sarah took the lead, chanting the incantations from their previous research. The symbols on the ground glowed with a brilliant light, resonating with the energy of the alignment.

As they performed the ritual, the rift's distortion intensified. The shimmering light grew brighter, and the air was filled with a low, resonant hum. The mansion's energy seemed to respond, as if drawing strength from the cosmic alignment.

Suddenly, the rift began to stabilize, and the distortion started to take on a more defined shape. From within the rift emerged a figure, cloaked in shimmering light. The figure appeared humanoid but radiated an otherworldly aura.

The trio stood their ground, their protective barriers in place. The figure stepped closer, its presence both mesmerizing and intimidating. It spoke in a voice that seemed to echo from beyond the stars.

"Greetings, seekers of balance," the figure said. "I am an emissary from the celestial realms. The alignment has allowed me to cross into your world. I come with a message and a warning."

Sarah, Liam, and Emma listened intently as the emissary continued. "The balance of cosmic forces is delicate, and the alignment has created a temporary bridge between worlds. While this rift is stable now, it is susceptible to disturbances. Your actions have helped maintain the balance, but further vigilance is required."

The emissary's eyes gleamed with a knowing light. "The cosmic forces are shifting, and the alignment will soon close. Yet, the energies you have worked with will leave a lasting impact. Be prepared for changes and challenges that may arise from the residual energies."

With a graceful gesture, the emissary began to fade, its form dissolving into the shimmering light of the rift. The rift itself began to close, the distortion in the air gradually vanishing as the alignment ended.

Sarah, Liam, and Emma watched in awe as the celestial spectacle faded, leaving them with a profound sense of accomplishment and responsibility. The rift had been managed, and the emissary's message had left them with much to consider.

As the first light of dawn began to break over the horizon, the trio descended from the hill, their minds filled with reflections on the night's events. The cosmic alignment had revealed a glimpse of the vastness and complexity of the universe, and they knew that their journey was far from over.

Raven Hollow awoke to a new day, its residents unaware of the celestial drama that had unfolded. For Sarah, Liam, and Emma, the experience had deepened their understanding of the magical and cosmic forces at play. The Harvest Moon had marked the beginning of their adventure, and the alignment had been a significant chapter in their ongoing exploration of the mysteries of the universe.

As they parted ways, each carrying their own reflections and insights, they knew that the future held both challenges and wonders. The echoes of their experiences would guide them, and the universe continued to beckon with its endless possibilities.

About the Author

Dear Reader,

Thank you for opening the pages of *Moonlit Convergence* and embarking on this mystical journey with Sarah, Liam, and Emma. Your curiosity and imagination are the lifeblood of this story, and it has been a pleasure to craft a world of magic, cosmic wonder, and adventure for you.

Every chapter was written with you in mind, hoping to transport you to a place where the ordinary meets the extraordinary, and where the boundaries of reality blur with the allure of the unknown. Your engagement with this tale is deeply appreciated, and it is your support and enthusiasm that make storytelling a truly magical endeavor.

As you close this book, I hope the echoes of Raven Hollow and the celestial mysteries linger with you, sparking dreams and inspiring new adventures. Thank you for being a part of this journey—your presence has made the experience all the more special.

With heartfelt gratitude,

Raven Penman